Douglas's Trousers

by Sarah Griffiths
Illustrated by Holly Bushnell

TEAMAUTHOR UK
Self-Publishing with you

To

Morgan,

With my very best
wishes,

Sarah
Griffiths

× ×
♡

For my beautiful Eva.
You are my inspiration
.
My gift to you is my love of stories and rhyme
for you to treasure forever.

Now little Douglas had been known,
To experiment with spells at home.

One day he had been in his loft,
With all the dust he'd coughed and coughed!

So how had these trousers come to be?
A magical garment to set Douglas free.

"Look up there," Maisie bellowed.
She pointed straight at the flying fellow.
"Miss Winter, quick, get him down!"
Soon the news would be all over town.

"Goodness, gosh, oh what to do?"
Miss Winter's face had turned quite blue.

But Douglas now had soared, then **ZIP**,
The trouser leg began to rip.

Caught on the top of a weather vane.
"Ow" and "ouch" and "eek" the pain!

Get him *down!*

Round and round the room they flew,
What was happening? No one knew!

As the boy went outside to play,
He felt his feet begin to sway.
From side to side the trousers heaved,
Up into the air, little Douglas weaved.

High above the old conker tree,
He banged and scraped and scratched his knee.

"Hey," he yelled,
"I'm up here!"
With not even one inch of fear.
"My trousers, my trousers!" Douglas screamed.
"This is fantastic," Douglas beamed.

Then all of a sudden, they began to glisten.
A little voice said, "Douglas, listen!"
"Put me on!" the trousers spoke.
Then whizz and bang and a cloud of smoke!

With a cough and wheeze
Douglas tried,
To put both of his legs inside.
They felt warm, cosy and tingly too.

The colour had changed
From black to blue.

When all the children had left the room,
Douglas thought, "I'll find them soon!"

As he pondered and looked around
A crumpled pile there he found.

Upon the floor the trousers moved,
Turned a little and then they zoomed.

One day at school,
Upon the floor,
Were Douglas's trousers
By the classroom door!

Dumped into a modest pile,
They had been that way a little while.

"Where are your trousers?"
The teacher cried!
"Get yourself changed,"
Miss Winter sighed.

He'd come across his grandad's box,
A treasure chest filled with socks.

But in the socks hidden away,
Were potions and recipes that say,

"In order to fly, you need some wings...
But failing that, then try these things."

"A single feather from a range of birds,
To normal folk, it seems absurd!
Geese and ducks and robins too,
An owl, a parrot, to name a few."

But I cannot divulge the whole lot,
In case you try out this outrageous plot!
I will however, let you know,
The secret ingredient below.

A sprinkle of eggshell from the curlew bird,
One of the rarest creatures in the world.

Douglas's grandad had liked to spot,
The finest birds...he'd seen the lot!

So now that I have begun to share,
Just how this boy had got up there,
It was quite a peculiar sight,
To see a child at such a height!

By now the whole school was out.
"Are you all right?" his friends did shout.
"I'm great, I'm free, I can see for miles."
But down below there were no smiles.

Huge crowds had begun to form,
Loud cheers and screams and sounds of horns.

The local news had heard what's what,
That Douglas Swift had got quite stuck!
"Today," the local newsreader began,
"A boy has flown like Peter Pan!"

"I'll get my ladder," the caretaker hollered.
With that, all of the parents followed.

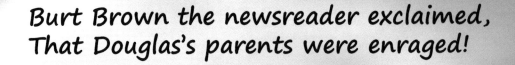

Burt Brown the newsreader exclaimed,
That Douglas's parents were enraged!

That their son had been allowed to leave,
The premises, they could not believe.

That now their son was flying high,
He'd left the roof and was in the sky.

"My little boy," Mrs Swift was shocked.
"He's getting away," Mr Swift had clocked!

Now Douglas had become quite pale,
He spotted the postman delivering mail.

And as he passed migrating geese,
He thought, "Well, I've missed maths at least!"

"Where are you taking me?" Douglas asked.
He breathed in deeply, sighed then gasped.

"I'm trying to help!" the trousers said.
Higher and higher Douglas was led.

Now what I have not begun to say
Is that the school was due to close that day.

A thriving, happy, little place,
Was being shut, a complete disgrace!

Douglas had written a letter,
To try and make the situation better.

But being forgetful, as he was,
It had been left in his trousers because...

Meow

He had forgotten to post it a week before,
Instead he'd discovered Grandad's potions in store.

The excitement of being able to fly,
Had taken priority of Douglas's eye!

On his hands the potion had tipped,
And into his pockets the liquid had slipped.

By true magic and wonder,
Beyond all hope,
The potion had worked
Outside all scope.

Now the media had arrived at this quiet country town,
To try and get poor Douglas down.

Because of this wondrous, peculiar sight,
The authorities had been given a terrible fright.

There were people with banners, shouting,
"Save our school!"
Hoping that justice would come to rule.

Quickly the news had spread world-wide,
Maybe there was a solution to find.

SAVE OUR SCHOOL

Children were interviewed and parents too.
"Please," they said, "is there anything you can do?"

"Saving Douglas is our main priority,"
Said Mr Fairfax the head of the local authority.

"Helicopters are on their way,
To save the boy, I hope and pray.
That he is safe and sound quite soon.
I feel that I have changed my tune."

"I have decided that I must declare,
To close the school was quite unfair."

The trousers flinched and jerked a bit,
They made poor Douglas feel quite sick.

"My job is done," the trousers cried.
"Hooray, Hoorah!" Douglas replied.

And now the boy came into view.
"Look," said Maisie... "The boy who flew!"

"I now propose that there must be
A brand new start, the school will see."

And softly, slowly, down he came.
"Oh Douglas, darling don't do that again!"
Mrs Swift in tears, hugged her boy,
And squeezed him tight with love and joy.

A little tale of magic and flight,
Of trousers that flew to a soaring height.

But without the support and love of the town,
Would little Douglas have ever come down?

So always practice what you preach,
And maybe magic isn't beyond your reach.

Acknowledgements

I would like to thank my wonderful husband Martyn for always believing in me and encouraging me to succeed with my passion for writing. You are my motivation and my endless support! Thank you for making me realise my true potential and helping make my dream a reality. I love you so very much.

Thank you to my beautiful daughter Eva.
You have such a love of stories and an infectious appetite for sharing your favourite books. I love to listen to you reading stories that you remember and rhyming the words together. You are my inspiration and have a knowledge beyond your years. It is this precious time together that I will treasure forever. I love you dearly and I am so proud to be able to share the stories I have written with you.

Thank you to my mum and dad for all the special time you spent reading to me when I was a little girl. This sparked an interest that has turned into my passion. Thank you for always believing in me. I love you.

Thank you to Sue Miller for all your help and advice to publish my first book. Thank you to Holly Bushnell for your magnificent illustrations. I can't thank you enough for bringing my characters to life. Thank you to all the team at Team Author UK for your help and support.

About the Author

Sarah is excited to have started her journey as a self-published children's author. She is a full-time mum to a 2-year-old daughter, taking a break from her job as a primary school teacher.

Reading and writing rhyming tales has always been a great passion of Sarah's. After becoming a mother, she realised her dream was to become a published children's author so her stories would come to life for daughter Eva.

Her stories have been inspired from children she has taught and places visited. Sarah's love of imagination and story writing came from reading Roald Dahl and Alan Ahlberg.

To follow Sarah and find out more about her books, please visit:

FB: https://www.facebook.com/SarahGriffithsAuthor/

http://twitter.com/SarahGriffithsA

About the Illustrator

Holly Bushnell is an artist and illustrator. She specialises in bespoke murals for schools, Nurseries, private commissions and bookshops. Holly is a member of TeamAuthorUK and is one of their children's illustrators.

Find out more about Holly at:

www.hollybushnelldesigns.co.uk

About the Author

Sarah is excited to have started her journey as a self-published children's author. She is a full-time mum to a 2-year-old daughter, taking a break from her job as a primary school teacher.

Reading and writing rhyming tales has always been a great passion of Sarah's. After becoming a mother, she realised her dream was to become a published children's author so her stories would come to life for daughter Eva.

Her stories have been inspired from children she has taught and places visited. Sarah's love of imagination and story writing came from reading Roald Dahl and Alan Ahlberg.

To follow Sarah and find out more about her books, please visit:

FB: https://www.facebook.com/SarahGriffithsAuthor/
T: http://twitter.com/SarahGriffithsA

About the Illustrator

Holly Bushnell is an artist and illustrator. She specialises in bespoke murals for schools, Nurseries, private commissions and bookshops. Holly is a member of TeamAuthorUK and is one of their children's illustrators.

Find out more about Holly at:

www.hollybushnelldesigns.co.uk

Made in the USA
Columbia, SC
18 October 2017